MR. LUNCH BORROWS A CANOE

BY J. otto SEIBOLD and VIVIAN WALSH
ILLUSTRATED BY J. otto SEIBOLD

VIKING

dedicated to: JOE and LINNELL

VIKING
Published by the Penguin Group
Penguin Books USA Inc., 375 Hudson Street, New York, New York 11014, U.S.A.
Penguin Books Ltd, 27 Wrights Lane, London W8 5TZ, England
Penguin Books Australia Ltd, Ringwood, Victoria, Australia
Penguin Books Canada Ltd, 10 Alcorn Avenue, Toronto, Ontario, Canada M4V 3B2
Penguin Books (N.Z.) Ltd, 182-190 Wairau Road, Auckland 10, New Zealand

Penguin Books Ltd, Registered Offices: Harmondsworth, Middlesex, England

First published in 1994 by Viking, a division of Penguin Books USA Inc.

10 9 8 7 6 5 4 3 2 1

Library of Congress Cataloging in Publication Data
Seibold, J. otto.
Mr. Lunch borrows a canoe/by J. otto Seibold and Vivian Walsh. p. cm.
Summary: When Mr. Lunch, canine bird chaser extraordinaire, sees a
bear while canoeing, he paddles so fast and so far that he ends up
in Venice.
ISBN 0-670-85661-4
[1. Dogs-Fiction. 2. Canoes and canoeing-Fiction.] I. Walsh,
Vivian, ill. II. Title.
PZ7.S45513Mo 1994 [E] dc20 94-10933 CIP AC

Text printed on recycled paper.

The illustrations in this book were created on an Apple Macintosh
computer using Adobe Illustrator software.

Printed in U.S.A.
Set in Times Roman and Arbitrary Bold

MR. LUNCH WAS VERY GOOD at CHASING BIRDS.  IN FACT, HE WAS A PROFESSIONAL.

Outside   Inside   at the Park

It was a very noisy day at Mr. Lunch's bird-chasing office. The birds had waited a whole year for this day. They were expecting a letter from an elephant.

When the mail finally arrived, the birds sat quietly as Mr. Lunch opened the special envelope. Mr. Lunch announced that there would be no work the following day, as everyone was invited to the Elephant Brand Bird Seed Company's annual picnic.

That evening the last bird to leave the office said, "See you by the free seeds, Mr. Lunch."

It was fine weather for a picnic. Mr. Lunch tried to organize a game of chase-the-bird, but the birds' beaks were too full of seeds for them to respond. The Bird Seed Company's president, a well-dressed elephant, waved Mr. Lunch over. The elephant told him about a canoe he had recently ordered from a catalog. Unfortunately, when the canoe arrived it was much too small for an elephant.

Then the elephant said, "Perhaps you would like to borrow it? You'd be surprised what a canoe can do for you."

Before Mr. Lunch could answer, the elephant made a quick trip out to his truck, and returned with the canoe. Mr. Lunch decided today was as good a day as any for a canoe ride. The elephant put a pair of protective water pants over his fancy clothes and then held the canoe steady for Mr. Lunch. Mr. Lunch hopped in and started down the river.

He could barely hear the elephant yelling "bon voyage," or possibly, "wrong way." Mr. Lunch was unconcerned. He had a canoe to drive.

The river was full of surprises.

Mr. Lunch spoke with a fish,

saw a bug's house,

and took a picture of an interesting bird.

Mr. Lunch had everything he needed to set up camp for the night. He didn't know that a few trees away there was someone watching him. A BEAR!

The bear was sure he'd seen that dog on television. He's that world-famous professional something-or-another, thought the bear. What *is* his name? The bear was determined to take a photograph of the famous celebrity.

But just as the bear snapped his shutter, Mr. Lunch jumped straight up and into his canoe.

Mr. Lunch was scared of bears.

Mr. Lunch
was very scared of
bears. He paddled as fast as he
could. What a big bear, he thought, and
paddled even faster. He paddled when he was
tired, and he kept on paddling when he was really
tired, until he wasn't sure if he was still paddling or just
dreaming that he was paddling.

Mr. Lunch awoke to the sound of voices. He opened his eyes one at a time, and saw a city that didn't look like any city he had ever seen before. This city had water where others had streets. In this town nobody noticed a dog in a boat, because everyone was in a boat.

Mr. Lunch saw many different types of boats.

CLOTHING boat

ROW boat

PERSONAL boat

TAXI boat

POLICE boat

WORK boat

the RUST BUCKET

Mr. Lunch had been in the canoe for a long time. He decided it was time to explore on foot. He came upon a vendor selling packets of bird seed. What luck! He bought some for the elephant (who collected bird seeds). Could this mean there were birds nearby? When Mr. Lunch turned the corner he found his answer.

He saw a large plaza full of pigeons. Mr. Lunch had never seen so many birds in one place before.

He certainly had never chased this many birds before. This would be the biggest bird-chasing challenge of his career. He formed a daring plan, took a deep breath, and expertly cleared the plaza.

Mr. Lunch stood in the center of the empty square. There wasn't a bird left; there wasn't a peep.

The silence that filled the square was so unusual that it woke up the street sweepers who were napping in nearby cafés. With the birds out of their way, they rushed in and began to sweep. When they finished, the plaza was clean, and no dirt could be seen.

A civic ceremony was quickly planned to honor Mr. Lunch. Thanks to him the plaza was spotless for the first time in years. A tuba played, as an official presented Mr. Lunch with the city's traditional gift of gratitude, the Golden Outboard Motor. Mr. Lunch was honored. He accepted the shiny prize and thanked those in attendance. One pigeon, Falconé, was so impressed with Mr. Lunch's bird-chasing that he asked to return with him as an apprentice.

With the Golden Outboard Motor attached to the canoe,
and Falconé (who was part homing pigeon) giving directions,
Mr. Lunch sped home.

When Mr. Lunch got back to his office he noticed that his trip had taken a toll on the borrowed canoe. This was no way to return something. Mr. Lunch always liked to return things looking as good as when he borrowed them, if not better. Mr. Lunch went to work.

When he was finished, Mr. Lunch was sure he had outdone himself. The canoe was now suitable for an elephant and ready to be returned. The Bird Seed Company president was at a loss for words to explain how he felt about the customized canoe.

SOUVENIR

SEEDS

Mr. Lunch thanked the elephant and gave
him the packet of souvenir seeds.

As the elephant floated away, Mr. Lunch knew
it was time to get back to what he loved best.